W9-BSB-835

Sunny Day

The Birthday Wish List!

Adapted by **Mickie Matheis**

Based on the screenplay **"Sunny's Birthday Wish List"** by **Jodi Reynolds**

Illustrated by **Miranda Yeo**

A Random House PICTUREBACK® Book

Random House 🏠 New York

rhcbooks.com
ISBN 978-1-5247-6852-2
Printed in the United States of America
10 9 8 7 6 5 4 3 2 1

"Surprise!" yelled Sunny's friends Rox and Blair and her adorable dog, Doodle, as Sunny walked through the door. They were decorating the salon for her birthday the next day.

Sunny smiled. "Oh, thanks! I love surprises, and decorating! Why don't we do it together?"

They had almost finished when Blair found Sunny's wish list book in the box of decorations.

"After my *last* birthday, I put together a wish list of all the things I wanted to try before *this* birthday," Sunny explained. She and her friends checked the list. It sure was long.

bake a cake

be a ballerina

ride a pony

be Queen for a day!

go fishing

play guitar

knit something

arrange flowers

"Now that there's only one day to go, I guess I won't be making those wishes come true," Sunny said sadly.

"Wait! Maybe if we help, we can make them happen," Blair suggested.

"I like it!" Rox said. "Think big! Dream big! Go big! Let's do this!"

Sunny slipped the wish list book into her pocket. "Ready, set, gear up, and go!"

The girls and Doodle piled into the Glam Van and headed for Cindy's Bakery.

Cindy and her kitten, Ralph, were happy to help with Sunny's birthday wish list. "I've never baked a cake on my own before," Sunny told her. "But I do really like eating it!"

Cindy showed Sunny, Rox, and Blair how to follow a recipe to bake their own cakes.

"And now the best part . . . ," said Cindy. "Decorating!"

"These cakes are great on their own, but they'd be even *better* if we put them together," Sunny decided. They stacked the three cakes to make one towering cake— and it looked awesome!

One birthday wish had come true!

The group then went to the park, where their friend Hannah and her ballet troupe were practicing.

"This is where we can make your ballerina birthday wish happen!" said Rox.

"But first you have to look the part!" said Hannah.

Soon Sunny was wearing a tutu and had her hair in a neat bun. "Now I feel like a real ballerina," she said.

Hannah showed Sunny some moves, but they weren't easy.
"Maybe you should do ballet Sunny-style," Doodle suggested.
Sunny thought that was a great idea! She and Doodle did their
own fun moves while the ballerinas gracefully glided behind
them. When the music ended, Sunny and Doodle collapsed to
the floor, exhausted and laughing.

Blair checked another wish off the list.

Next, they went to the boardwalk to see Johnny-Ray and his pony, Suzette. They were happy to help make another of Sunny's birthday wishes come true.

Sunny climbed onto the pony. Riding Suzette was just as hard as ballet dancing. With Suzette's first few steps, Sunny almost bounced right off!

Sunny reached into her apron and pulled out some supplies. Hair ties tethered her to the saddle. A claw clip helped her hold on, too. And a ribbon tied her riding helmet to her head extra tight.

Soon Sunny was riding and having a wonderful time. Another wish was fulfilled!

The friends spent the rest of the afternoon finishing Sunny's wish list. Annabella and Dominica crowned her queen for the day.

She went fishing with her friends.

She arranged flowers,

knitted,

and even played guitar!

The girls and Doodle returned to Sunny's Salon. They were so excited to have finished the wish list book! But as Sunny closed it, a piece of paper slipped out.

"It looks like you've got one wish left," said Doodle. It was a drawing of a circle.

"It's the moon," Sunny said. "It's always been one of my biggest wishes to visit the moon!"

"The moon is far away," noted Blair. "We'd need a spaceship and space suits."

"We're sorry, Sunny," said Rox. "We wanted to make everything on your Wish List come true."

"That's okay," replied Sunny. "I did everything else, thanks to you. And I know there's no way I can *really* go to the moon." She hopped out of the van and went into the salon.

"Sunny *never* gives up," Doodle reminded the others.
"No matter how hard a problem is."

Suddenly, Rox had an idea—a BIG idea! If they were going
to pull it off, they would need help from all their friends.

That evening, Rox raced into the salon and pulled Sunny outside. Blair was waiting by the Glam Van. "Welcome aboard flight Happy Birthday, Sunny," she said.

Doodle was behind the wheel, wearing a helmet and a silver cloak. "We are cleared for liftoff!"

The girls strapped a very puzzled Sunny into the hair chair as Doodle counted down. "Three . . . two . . . one . . . BLASTOFF!"

The Glam Van took off down the road.

They drove until they came to the woods at the edge of Friendly Falls. "We have touchdown," Doodle said as he brought the van to a halt.

"Thank you for traveling on Doodle's Rocket Ship."

The girls got out of the van and followed Doodle toward an enormous rock.

It was so tall that it seemed to touch the sky.
Doodle scampered along a path winding up the
rock, and the girls hurried after him. At the top
was an amazing surprise.

"It's your very own moon-themed birthday party!"
Rox announced.

"Happy birthday!" Sunny's friends cheered.

The ground had been raked to look like the moon's surface, complete with craters. Colored balls hung from the trees like little planets. And at the center of it all was Sunny's cake, now decorated with a pretty moon and gold stars.

"Thanks, everyone, for making my birthday wishes come true," Sunny said. "I really feel like I'm on the moon!"

"I just wish there were some stars out tonight," Blair said.

Sunny knew how to make that wish come true.

She pulled a brush, some hair ties, and some bobby pins from her apron and went to work on her hair. After a few minutes, she turned around so everyone could see.

"It's my Night Sky Star Braid," Sunny said. "I've been saving it for the day I went to the moon—and today's that day! It's one for the Style Files!"

Sunny decided that this was officially her best birthday ever.

"It's not over yet," Rox said, guiding her to the edge of the rock.

The moon, huge and glowing, rose right in front of them.

"It's the best view in Friendly Falls," Blair pointed out.

"We know it's not the same as actually going to the moon," Rox said.

"No, it's even better," said Sunny. "Because this way, I get to share it with all my friends."